DETROIT PUBLIC LIBRARY

3 5674 01835797 1

D1537955

DETROIT PUBLIC LIBRARY

CHILDREN'S LIBRARY

DATE DUE

JUL 0 5 1995

JUL 0 5 1995

AUG 9 - 1995

SEP 2 2 1995

OCT 2 5 1995

OCT 2 5 1995

AUG 1 0 1999

Mole & Shrew Step Out

Mole & Shrew
Step Out

⤜ Jackie French Koller ⤛
illustrated by Stella Ormai

ATHENEUM   1992   NEW YORK

Maxwell Macmillan Canada
Toronto
Maxwell Macmillan International
New York   Oxford   Singapore   Sydney

Text copyright © 1992 by Jackie French Koller
Illustrations copyright © 1992 by Stella Ormai

All rights reserved. No part of this book may be reproduced or
transmitted in any form or by any means, electronic or mechanical,
including photocopying, recording, or by any information storage
and retrieval system, without permission in writing from the Publisher.

Atheneum
Macmillan Publishing Company
866 Third Avenue
New York, NY 10022

Maxwell Macmillan Canada, Inc.
1200 Eglinton Avenue East
Suite 200
Don Mills, Ontario M3C 3N1

Macmillan Publishing Company is part of the
Maxwell Communication Group of Companies.

First edition
Printed in Hong Kong
10 9 8 7 6 5 4 3 2 1
The text of this book is set in 16-point Goudy Oldstyle.
The illustrations are rendered in watercolors.

Library of Congress Cataloging-in-Publication Data
Koller, Jackie French.
Mole and Shrew step out/by Jackie French Koller.
p.   cm.
Summary: Mole commits a comic blunder regarding a fancy ball, but
his good friend Shrew sticks by him.
ISBN 0-689-31713-1
[1. Balls (Parties)—Fiction. 2. Moles (Animals)—Fiction.
3. Shrews—Fiction. 4. Friendship—Fiction.] I. Title.
PZ7.K833Mp 1992
[E]—dc20 91-20531

To Jared, Maegan, and Nicole, with love
—J.F.K.

To my daughters, Angelia and Maya. Love
—S.O.

Mole was out for his afternoon stroll. He stopped to chat with Shrew just as the postman arrived.

"Oh, it's here, it's here!" shrieked Shrew.

"Of course it's here," said Mole. "The mail comes every day."

"Not the mail," said Shrew, "my invitation to the ball." She held up a blue envelope with silver writing.

"The ball?" asked Mole. "What ball?"

"The ball at Mouse Manor," said Shrew. "It is *the* social event of the year, and *everybody* who is *anybody* is invited."

Shrew hugged her invitation dreamily, then glided up the walk and into her house.

Mole stared after her. "Everybody who is *anybody*?" he repeated. Suddenly he dashed off toward home. He arrived just as the postman was pulling away. Mole looked into his mailbox.

It was empty.

"Wait!" he cried, running after the postman. "Please wait!"

The postman stopped and turned around.

"Isn't there a blue envelope with silver writing for me?" asked Mole.

The postman looked through a fat pack of blue envelopes.

"No," he said. "No blue envelope for Mole."

"Oh, dear," said Mole. He turned away and walked slowly home.

Mole looked at himself in his front hall mirror.
"Hello, Mole," he said.
Nobody answered.
"Oh, dear," said Mole.
He yelled his name out the front door.
Nobody came.
He called louder.
Still, nobody came.

Mole rushed outside and ran all the way to Shrew's house.
He banged on her door.

"Shrew," he begged breathlessly, "may I use your phone?"

"Why, of course," said Shrew. "Is something wrong?"

"I'm afraid so," said Mole.

He dialed his own number.

"Oh dear, oh dear," he mumbled.

"Whatever is the matter?" asked Shrew.

"I just called myself up," said Mole, "and *nobody*
answered!"

Shrew looked at him oddly. "So?" she said.

"Don't you see?" said Mole. "*I'm* nobody!"

Shrew took the phone out of Mole's hand. "Mole," she said, "whatever are you talking about?"

"I didn't get an invitation to the ball," said Mole, "so I can't be *anybody*, and I spoke to myself in the mirror and nobody answered, then I called myself in the yard and nobody came, and now nobody answered my phone. Oh dear, oh dear." He put his head down between his hands and heaved a great sigh.

Shrew smiled and gently patted Mole's shoulder.

"Mole," she said, "of course you are somebody. Perhaps you didn't get an invitation because you've just moved into the neighborhood. Mouse hasn't met you yet. You shall go to the ball, as *my* guest."

"Really?" said Mole.

"Really," said Shrew. "Pick me up tonight at eight, and remember to wear a black tie and tails."

"Oh, thank you, thank you," said Mole, nearly falling out the door in his relief at being somebody after all.

He sauntered home, humming happily to himself, "Tonight at eight, black tie and tails, black tie and tails..."

Suddenly he stopped in his tracks.

"Tails?" he repeated to himself out loud. "Tails?"

He looked forlornly over his shoulder. He had only one tail, and it was a short, stubby thing at that.

"Oh, dear," Mole groaned again. Where was he to find some suitable tails by eight o'clock?

Just then he heard a sound, a hearty *slap, slap, slap*. It was Beaver, working down at the brook. Beaver had a wonderful tail, a magnificent tail.

Mole hurried down to the brook.

"Pardon me," he said to Beaver. "I wondered if I might borrow your tail?"

Beaver stopped his work and stared at Mole.

"Are you *mad*?" he asked gruffly.

"Mad?" repeated Mole. "Oh, no, not at all, I'm in a very good mood actually, or at least I was, until this whole tail business came up."

"You *are* mad," said Beaver with a snort.

"No, I'm not, really I'm not!"

But Beaver had dived under the water and disappeared.

"Humph," said Mole. "Perhaps I was too direct."

"Got a problem?" he heard someone ask.

Mole looked up. Lizard was sunning himself on a nearby rock.

"Oh," said Mole. "Not really. It's just that my tail is so puny, and it won't do at all, and besides, I only have one."

"How many does a body need?" asked Lizard. "One has always served me well enough."

"Well, I'm not sure," said Mole. "Two at least, maybe more. It's Mouse's party, you see, and Shrew didn't say."

Lizard shook his head. "Sounds like a bunch of hogwash," he said, "but if it means that much to you, take mine."

"Do you mean it?" said Mole.

"Of course I mean it. I can always grow another." And with a sudden snap Lizard disconnected his tail and handed it to Mole.

"Oh, thank you, thank you," said Mole; then he thought a moment. "How soon *could* you grow a new one?" he asked.

"A week or two," said Lizard.

"Oh," said Mole sadly. "I'm afraid that isn't soon enough."

"Look there," said Lizard. "Isn't that a kite?"

"Indeed it is," said Mole.

"And doesn't it have a tail?"

"Indeed it does!" said Mole. "Oh, thank you again, Lizard. You have been a great help."

Mole found the kite attached to a string, which was
attached to a very small frog.

"Pardon me," said Mole, "but I wondered if I might
borrow your kite tail?"

Frog looked up at Mole with large eyes. "But my kite
won't fly without it," he said.

"I only need it for tonight," said Mole, "and I'll take very
good care of it. I wouldn't ask if it wasn't *very* important."

Frog hung his head. "Well, all right, then," he said, "if it's *very* important."

He pulled his kite in and gave the tail to Mole.

"Thank you," said Mole. "I'll have it back first thing in the morning. I promise." He tucked the kite tail under his arm along with Lizard's. "I do hope two is enough," he mumbled. "It would be nice to have one more, just to be safe."

"One more what?" asked a high, thin voice.

Mole looked up. Worm was perched in a branch overhead.

"One more tail," said Mole. "I'm in need of tails."

"Sit down, then," said Worm, "and I'll spin you one. I'm a great spinner of tales."

Mole sat down and Worm began to spin the most wondrous tale of kings and queens and sailing ships, and far-off castles by the sea, and all the while she talked, she danced and whirled, and when she was done she handed Mole a tail of shining silk.

"Thank you. Thank you all!" Mole shouted to his new friends as he hurried home with his treasures in hand. "Someday I'll return the favor. You'll see."

Mole washed and dressed. It was getting late. He wound
his beautiful silk tail around his head like a hat. He tied his
kite tail around his waist like a belt. He hung Lizard's tail
from the belt, and he tied his black tie around his neck.

"Oh, my," he said, looking in the mirror. "I do look fine."

He strutted over and arrived at Shrew's door just shortly before eight.

When Shrew saw him, her eyes widened and her mouth dropped open.

"I knew I looked fine," said Mole, "but I didn't think you'd be speechless."

Shrew could only shake her head. "But, Mole," she stammered.

"No time to talk," said Mole. "It's getting late."

When they arrived at Mouse Manor, the butler was speechless too. Mole beamed with pride.

There was a sudden hush when they walked into the room. "Mercy!" shrieked Mouse.

Mole looked around. All the male guests were wearing penguin suits.

"You didn't tell me it was a costume ball," Mole whispered to Shrew. "You said to wear tails."

"Those aren't costumes," whispered Shrew. "They are tuxedos. They are called tails for short. I'm sorry. I thought you knew."

Suddenly Mole felt foolish. The guests were starting to snicker and laugh. "Excuse me," he said, bowing to Mouse. "I just remembered. It's my bowling night."

Then he dashed out of the house as fast as he could.

Mole sat down on a log. He felt awful, simply awful. He could never face his neighbors again.

"May I sit down too?"

Mole looked up. It was Shrew.

"You'll soil your beautiful gown," he said.

"I don't care," said Shrew.

She sat down next to Mole.

"You're missing the ball," said Mole.

"It's a very stuffy ball anyway," said Shrew. "I'd rather be with you."

"You're a good friend," said Mole.

"So are you," said Shrew. "In fact, I think we ought to have a ball of our own—a Good Friends' Ball."

"Oh," said Mole, "what a wonderful idea! Do you think we could invite Lizard and Frog and Worm?"

"Of course we can. We'll invite all our friends and we'll make sure nobody is left out."

Mole was quiet.

"Is something wrong, Mole?" asked Shrew.

"Well," said Mole. "Couldn't we invite nobody too? I hate to see anyone left out."

Shrew laughed. "Yes, dear Mole," she said. "We shall have the first party where *nobody* is invited, and *everyone* has a ball!"